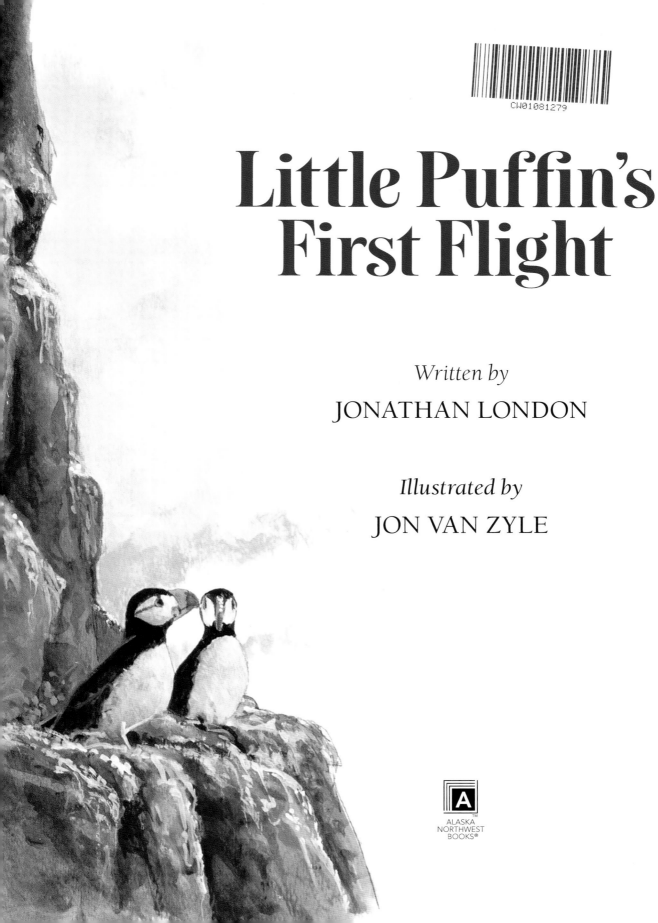

Little Puffin's First Flight

Written by

JONATHAN LONDON

Illustrated by

JON VAN ZYLE

ALASKA
NORTHWEST
BOOKS®

It's spring on the coast of Alaska.
After four years living at sea,
two puffins greet off the shore
of a snow-crusted island.

It's time to raise a chick!

They nuzzle their beautiful bills
and clap them gently together.
The puffins mate at sea.

Then, on a rocky slope
high up on the island, they dig a burrow
with their sharp beaks and claws.
They line the nest with feathers and grass.

Now it is ready.

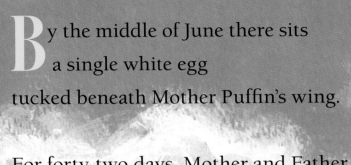

By the middle of June there sits
a single white egg
tucked beneath Mother Puffin's wing.

For forty-two days, Mother and Father
Puffin take turns keeping their fragile egg
warm while the other dives for food.

Finally, in the cliff-top nest,
there's a **tap! tap! tap!**

Then a jagged crack.
A beak pokes through.
The shell splits open . . .

and out steps a hungry gray fuzz-ball
*peep-peep-peep*ing for food.

It's Little Puffin!

His mother nuzzles his tiny beak—
but where is Father Puffin?

Here he is!
And his large bill is filled with fish
for Little Puffin.

Now it's Mother Puffin's turn to dive for food
while Father Puffin guards the burrow
from bald eagles, falcons, and squawking gulls.

Dressed in her life jacket
of carefully fluffed feathers,
Mother Puffin bobs like a cork
in the icy cold ocean.

Then, pressing the air out of her feathers . . .

... she flies underwater

With her heavy, almost solid bones,
she dives deep and deeper.

And with her big, colorful beak
she's the clown of the ocean,
doing underwater acrobatics
while swiftly chasing fish.

If she's lucky she'll swim back up,
her beak filled with small fish.

But high on the grassy cliffs
hungry predators await.
And when Mother Puffin lands . . .

Swooooosh!

A large gull grabs her in its beak
and shakes her . . .
'til she drops her whole catch!

Dazed but unharmed,
Mother Puffin dives deep and deeper
into the rolling sea to try again.

For six weeks, Mother and Father Puffin
take turns feeding Little Puffin.
But sometimes he's impatient.

He waits and waits
at the mouth of the burrow,
flapping his scrawny wings.

At last, when his wing feathers have finally
all grown in . . .

It is time!

One night,
when the gulls and eagles are all asleep,
Little Puffin stumble-jumps
out of his burrow
for the very first time.

He waddles in the moonlight—

wibble-wobble

wibble-wobble

to the edge of the rocky cliff.

He is all alone.

Little Puffin takes a step,
leaps into the air and . . .

tumbles over the cliff!

Flapping and flailing,
he plummets

down . . .

down . . .

down.

Just as he's about to crash into the sea,
Little Puffin spreads his wings . . .

and takes off!

Skimming across the moonlit waves,
he triumphantly rises . . .

and sails out to sea.

Sea Parrot.

Underwater Acrobat.

Clown of the Ocean.

Until, at four years old,
he will greet his own mate
and gently nuzzle her beautiful beak—
for it's spring on the coast of Alaska . . .

. . . and it's time to raise a chick!

Author's Note

The stars of this story are Horned Puffins, one of three species (the others are Atlantic and Tufted Puffins). Horned Puffins are members of the auk family and live in the cold waters of the North Pacific Ocean. Their unique look and swimming skills have earned them many nicknames: Sea Parrot, Underwater Acrobat, Clown of the Ocean.

Though they can fly, puffins are more at home in the water than in the air or on the land. Their short wings and heavy bones make it difficult for them to take off, and once in the air, they must flap 300 to 400 times per minute to keep themselves aloft!

But those heavy bones and stubby wings do make puffins excellent divers. They mostly dive for small fish, like capelin or herring, but they also catch squid, crabs, and jellyfish. Puffins can dive down over 200 feet and stay under for over two minutes. They have hinged beaks and spines on their tongues, which make it possible for them to carry ten or more fish at a time (the record is sixty-two!). It's a good thing, too, because a chick—or *puffling*—will eat as many as 2,000 fish in its first six weeks of life! Fortunately, puffins lay only one egg at a time. Parents must work almost full time to catch enough food for that one hungry chick.

But not all the fish they catch make it to the nest. Larger birds, including gulls, ravens, peregrine falcons, and snowy owls, often try to steal their catch. These birds, and bald eagles too, will snatch a puffling that strays outside its burrow. Other predators include arctic and red foxes, as well as rats. This is why one puffin parent always stays behind at the nest: to guard the puffling while the other dives for food.

Once a chick's feathers grow in (at around six weeks), however, its parents leave. No more guarding or feeding. Driven by hunger, the fledgling takes its first flight alone, then stays at sea for two to five years. Dull gray in the winter, some come back brightly colored in the spring and hang out in "clubs" with other young puffins, looking for a future mate. At four or five years old, this beautiful seabird is ready to start a family of its own. Most puffins mate for life and use the same nest site every year.

Although Horned Puffins are not endangered, their numbers are dropping due to pollution, the use of gill nets for fishing, and the decline of their prey fish. They are protected in Alaska, but not in British Columbia, Oregon, Washington, or California, where they spend the winter. Indeed, these delightful and colorful Clowns of the Ocean are becoming an increasingly rare sight.

Acknowledgments

Heartfelt thanks to Holly Hogan, Manager of the Witless Bay Ecological Reserve in Newfoundland, with whom—by special permit—my wife and I spent a cold, windy, grand day on Gull Island amidst those cousins of the Horned Puffins, the Atlantic Puffins, off the opposite shores of North America.

For Stephi and Sean, and sweet Maureen. With a special thanks to Holly Hogan, ecologist and puffin expert.
—Jonathan London

For Jonathan, it's always a pleasure to paint your words.
—Jon Van Zyle

LIBRARY OF CONGRESS CATALOGING-IN-PUBLICATION DATA
London, Jonathan, 1947-
Little Puffin's first flight / written by Jonathan London ; illustrated by Jon Van Zyle.
pages cm
Summary: Follows a family of puffins from the time the parents greet one another off the coast of Alaska and prepare to raise a family, through the care of their fragile egg and ravenous chick, to Little Puffin's first flight across and into the sea. Includes facts about puffins.
ISBN 978-0-88240-924-5 (pbk.)
ISBN 978-1-941821-40-4 (hardcover)
ISBN 978-1-941821-56-5 (e-book)
1. Horned puffin—Juvenile fiction. [1. Horned puffin—Fiction. 2. Puffins—Fiction. 3. Animals—Infancy—Fiction.] I. Van Zyle, Jon, illustrator. II. Title.
PZ10.3.L8534Lhk 2015
[E]—dc23
2014034763

Edited by Michelle McCann
Designed by Vicki Knapton and Jon Van Zyle

Published by Alaska Northwest Books® An imprint of

GRAPHIC ARTS BOOKS®

P.O. Box 56118
Portland, Oregon 97238-6118
503-254-5591
www.graphicartsbooks.com

Printed in China